LITTLE CRITTER MERRY CHRISTMAS

BY MERCER MAYER

Random House 🏠 **New York**

Little Critter Merry Christmas book, characters, text, and images © 2013 Mercer Mayer. Little Critter, Mercer Mayer's Little Critter, and Mercer Mayer's Little Critter and Logo are registered trademarks of Orchard House Licensing Company. All rights reserved. Published in the United States by Random House Children's Books, a division of Random House, Inc., 1745 Broadway, New York, NY 10019, and in Canada by Random House of Canada Limited, Toronto. Random House and the colophon are registered trademarks of Random House, Inc. The material contained in this book was taken from the following Golden Books publications: *Just for You*, copyright © 1975 Mercer Mayer, and *Merry Christmas Mom and Dad*, copyright © 1983 Mercer Mayer.

randomhouse.com/kids

ISBN 978-0-375-97297-3

Printed in the United States of America

10 9 8 7 6 5 4 3 2 1

MERRY ~~KRIS~~ CHRISTMAS MOM and DAD

BY MERCER MAYER

wanted to make
Christmas very special
just for you,
so I made a Christmas wreath.

I wanted to decorate
some Christmas cookies
just for you,
but I couldn't stop
tasting them.

I wanted to find a Christmas present just for you,
but there were too many toys to look at.

So I asked Santa to bring you
a special present instead.

I wanted to wrap
the baby's present
just for you,

but the tape was too sticky.

I picked out a Christmas tree
just for you...

but it was too big
to take home.

I wanted to carry
the Christmas balls
just for you,

but the box was upside down.

So I got out
the Christmas lights,
but they were
all tangled.

I wanted to put the star
on top of our tree
all by myself…so Dad helped.

On Christmas Eve
I tried to go right to sleep
just for you,

but I was too excited.

I didn't want to make you get up
too early on Christmas morning…

JUST FOR ~~YU~~ YOU

BY MERCER MAYER

This morning I wanted
to make breakfast just for you...
but the eggs
were too slippery.

I wanted to wash the floor
just for you,
but the soap was too bubbly.

I wanted to put away the dishes
just for you,
but the floor was too wet.

I wanted to carry the groceries
just for you,
but the bag broke.

I ate my sandwich
just for you,
but not my crusts.

I wanted to take a nap
just for you,
but the bed was too bouncy.

I wanted to mow the lawn
just for you,
but I was too little.

I picked an apple
just for you,
but on the way home
I got hungry.

I wanted to set the table
just for you,
but the TV was too loud.

I wanted to
not splash in my bath
just for you...

...but there was a storm.

I wanted to do something very special,

just for you.

And I did it.

© Mercer Mayer

© Mercer Mayer